BIGMOUTH

by Maggie Twohill

Bradbury Press

NEW YORK

Bradbury Press
An Affiliate of Macmillan, Inc.
866 Third Avenue, New York, N.Y. 10022
Collier Macmillan Canada, Inc.
Manufactured in the United States of America
1 3 5 7 9 10 8 6 4 2
The text of this book is set in 12 pt. Caledonia.

Library of Congress Cataloging-in-Publication Data
Twohill, Maggie. Bigmouth.
Summary: A well-intentioned young girl, who talks more
than she listens, garbles a message from her father's boss
leading the family to think they are moving to London.
[1. Communication—Fiction.   2. conduct of life—fiction]
I. Title.   PZ7.T93Bi 1986 [Fic]   86-12889
ISBN 0-02-789260-3

6-30-87
10.95
B+T
Jfic
.C#1

BIGMOUTH

1

Bunny Squill plopped down at the kitchen table, took a bite of an oatmeal cookie, gulped a swig of milk, and went on talking.

"—so as soon as the teacher called on her, I raised my hand, 'cause I *knew* she was going to say 'Chicago,' I just knew it, and sure enough, she—"

"Bunny, just stop long enough to have your cookies and milk, all right?" her mother asked tiredly. "My head is really spinning right now . . ."

Mrs. Squill taught nursery school. Three-year-olds in the mornings, four-year-olds in the afternoons. When she got home, she spoke in whispers, and often pressed her forehead with the thumb and pinkie of her right hand.

Bunny swallowed more milk. "Sorry, Mom, I'll talk softer. So anyway, sure enough, she said *Chicago* is the capital of Illinois—*everyone* says that, right? Why do you think that is? Probably because Chicago is a famous big city and you hardly *ever* hear anything about Springfield, even though it's—"

"Listen, Bunny—"

"So I quick raised my hand, because I *knew* Springfield was the answer, not Chicago, and I waved it and waved it, but Mrs. Pinfish wouldn't even—"

"Bunny—"

"—call on me. She hardly ever, *ever* calls on me and I *always* know the answer. Why is that, Mom?"

Mrs. Squill was holding her forehead between her thumb and pinkie.

"Mom, why is it that Mrs. Pinfish hardly ever calls on me? Why do you think? Mom? Did you hear me?"

"No . . ."

"Because I always know the answer and even more lots of times. Like, for example, Springfield? I knew that Abraham Lincoln lived there for twenty-five years! Geraldine didn't know that. Helen didn't know that. Mary Ann didn't—"

"Bunny!"

"What?"

Mrs. Squill continued to hold her head, and while she talked she closed her eyes. "Bunny, the new little girl in the morning class cried steadily for three hours until her mother picked her up."

"Uh-huh . . ."

"And in the four-year-old class, two boys and a girl had a contest to see who could hit the highest note."

"Uh-huh . . ."

"Another little girl found the old drum set in the storage closet, and I couldn't tear her away from it—"

"Uh-huh?"

"—and I have heard quite enough noises for one day. Bunny, do you understand what I'm saying? Because it hurts me just to have spoken those words." Now she held her head with both hands.

"I'm sorry, Mom," Bunny said.

"Thank you."

"I think maybe you should switch to teaching older kids. After all, you know how little kids are. They make noise all day long. Either they're screaming at each other or banging on blocks or giggling so hard you can hardly—"

"*Bunny!*" Mrs. Squill cried, and then added softly, "Ow." She began to rub her temples.

"Sorry, Miz Lucy," Bunny teased. She knew the children called her mother "Miz Lucy" because "Mis-sus Squill" was too difficult for most of them to arrange in their small mouths. Especially the ones with lisps.

"Bunny, why don't you go out and play?" her mother suggested.

Bunny sniffed. "I went out and played *last* year. When I was in *fourth* grade. Now that I've started fifth I'm too old to go out and play."

"Then . . . then . . . just go out and *don't* play," her mother moaned.

"Where's Freddy?" Bunny asked. Freddy Junior was her sixteen-year-old brother.

"He's out," Mrs. Squill replied. "He's probably at his new girlfriend's house."

"Yeah," Bunny agreed. "He re-eeally likes her. Her name is Marvelle Maloney and she lives over on Rivermont Road, right near the fire station where they have that big field and every year the carnival—"

"Bunny . . ."

"All right." Bunny got up from the table. "I have to call Ruthie anyway. We were going to make plans to give Helen a surprise party and we couldn't do it in school since Helen's always around, so we decided to get together *after*—"

"Bunny!"

"I'm going, I'm go-ing . . . "
Lucy Squill sighed a long sigh.

"Hi, Ruthie, it's me!"

"Bunny?"

"Uh-huh. Did you just get home?"

"Yes, but—"

"Me, too. But I had time for a snack. Listen, is now a good time to plan Helen's party? I thought I'd come on over to your house now, okay?"

"Well, it was, but—"

"I wanted my brother, Freddy, to drive me in his new car. I mean, it isn't *really* new—in fact, it's falling apart—but he says he can keep it running with his magic touch."

"Bunny, look—"

"The best part is, it's a convertible, so we can all ride with the top down. I mean, we *have* to ride with the top down because it doesn't have a top right now, but Freddy says he'll put one on before it gets cold. After all, it's September, so how cold can it get? But he's at his girlfriend's, so—"

"Bunny!"

"What?"

"Just stop talking a minute, okay?"

"Uh-huh . . . "

"Helen's *here!*"

"What? I can't hear you when you whisper, Ruthie...."

"I said, Helen's *here!* She just dropped over. So how can we plan her party if she's here?"

"Can't you make her go home? Make her go home, Ruthie. Get rid of her!"

"Okay, I'll try, Bunny. You get Geraldine and I'll see what I can do about getting Helen to leave. I'll call Mary Ann and—"

"Geraldine?"

"Huh?"

"Did you say for me to get Geraldine?"

"Sure. You do live on the same street, don't you?"

"Yes..."

"Well, what's the problem? I'll see what I can do with Helen. You come over. Okay, Bunny?"

"Okay...'bye." Bunny hung up. "*Ger*-aldine," she muttered to herself. "Oh, all right..." She called Geraldine and arranged to meet her on the way to Ruthie's.

Bunny was happiest when she was talking. And she was happy most of the time. When she was younger, she talked to herself if no one was around. Or she talked to her dolls or to people on television or to the neighbor's dog. Her parents, Lucy and

Freddy Senior, considered it cute, the way Bunny talked to everything. Sometimes they'd stand in the doorway of her room at night when it was dark and she didn't know they were there. They'd smile to themselves as Bunny chattered away in her bed, recounting her day to her teddy bear.

Now that Bunny was older and still talking a blue streak, Freddy Senior and Lucy Squill no longer stood outside their daughter's door each night to listen to her. Now they tilted their heads at each other in the lovely silence that followed after their daughter was tucked away upstairs at bedtime. Still, they were glad she was such a helpful, friendly person. . . .

Now when there was no one to talk to, Bunny sang to herself. If she didn't know the words to the songs Freddy Junior blared on his radio, she made up her own words. Bunny's songs were about her friends in Opata Park, her teachers, her brother and his girlfriends, her father and his job at the Burnside & Burnside advertising agency, her mother and *her* job at the Opata Park Playschool.

As she skipped down her street, her high soprano voice babbled a tune about her brother's latest girl-friend. Her thick curly brown hair bobbed up and down against the back of her neck in rhythm with the song.

"Mar-vel-ous Mar-velle, Fred-dy thinks she's

swell," Bunny sang. "She's got long blond hair and is ve-ry fair. . . . She has a little dog and I think he's nice, but he bit my broth-er twi-i-ce. . . ."

Suddenly another girl blocked Bunny's path. Bunny raised her head in time to stop herself from running into her.

"Hi, Bunny," the girl said. "Did I interrupt a conversation with yourself?"

Bunny wasn't embarrassed. "No, Geraldine," she answered, "I was singing. I hope Ruthie was able to get Helen to go home, don't you? Otherwise we'll never find time by ourselves to plan her surprise party."

"I hope we can make a really nice party," Geraldine said as they fell into step together. "I hope it's one Helen will always remember." She looked up and smiled. "Look," she said. "There's the Pennywhistle Lane street sign."

"*I* know," Bunny said. "I live here, too. On Pennywhistle Lane. I always have, same as you, Geraldine. I grew up here, same as you."

"Yes, but your last name isn't Pennywhistle, like mine. Your street wasn't named for you."

"It wasn't named for you, either, Geraldine. It was named for your great-grandfather. You just happened to be born with his last name, that's all. And you know, if your great-grandfather had daughters instead of sons, and then your *grand*father had daughters instead of sons, then your name wouldn't even *be* Pennywhistle! It would be the name of whoever your *mother* married, instead of your—"

"I know, Bunny, I know, but—"

"I mean, I guess your grandmother *and* your mother could have kept the name 'Pennywhistle' if they wanted to, because lots of women do that now, but—"

"Bunny—"

"But not *then*, they didn't. They always took their husband's—"

"Bunny!" Geraldine clapped her hand over Bunny's mouth. Wide eyes stared at Geraldine over the hand.

"Now listen, Bunny, I don't *care* who takes whose name! My great-grandfather had a *son* and he was my *grandfather*! And *he* had a son and that was my *father*! There weren't any *daughters*, so my name *is* Pennywhistle, just like theirs! And I'm proud of it because my great-grandfather was this town's first *mayor*, so our street is named for him, *okay*?" She took her hand away from Bunny's mouth and wiped it on her jeans. "I hate doing that, Bunny, but you never shut up!"

"Okay," Bunny said, and continued walking. "Okay, I know your great-grandfather was the first mayor. Everybody knows that, Geraldine. . . ."

"Okay, then."

"But you're not the only one with a famous ancestor, you know."

"Oh, sure. Everybody knows about the first President of the United States, President *Squill!*" Geraldine giggled.

"I never said 'President,' " Bunny sniffed. "Besides, maybe *my* great-grandfather had daughters!"

"Okay," Geraldine sighed.

"I'm sure," Bunny went on, "that somewhere back there I had an ancestor who . . . " She went on chattering until they reached Ruthie Walcott's house on Opata Drive. Ruthie answered their knock.

"She's gone!" Ruthie said gleefully. "She had to go home to clean her room. Mary Ann's here, and we have till suppertime to plan a really terrific party!"

"Oh, good!" Geraldine cried as she and Bunny stepped into the Walcotts' living room. "Oh, hi, Mary Ann," she called as a girl with a bouncing pony tail came toward them.

"Ruthie and I were discussing some ideas for the party," Mary Ann said. "You know, decorations and things . . . "

"Did I tell you about my brother's car?" Bunny asked as she flopped on Ruthie's sofa.

"Of course you did," Mary Ann answered.

"Did I tell you he bought it from Herbie Farnsworth after Herbie graduated last June? It's really a heap, but it only cost Freddy a hundred dollars. He painted it—"

"Bunny, we're here to talk about the party," Geraldine said.

"—red and yellow," Bunny went on. "It coughs when it runs, but it's really fun to ride in, just like the roller coaster at—"

"Bunny!" Ruthie reached out and clapped her hand over Bunny's mouth. Geraldine and Mary Ann did the same, their hands landing on top of Ruthie's. The three girls held tight.

"Now listen, Bunny—are you listening?" Ruthie asked.

Bunny nodded. The girls' hands jerked up and down with the nod.

"Okay. Now the four of us are here to plan Helen's surprise birthday party. Right?"

A nod from Bunny. Three hands moved up and down.

"Okay. No more about Freddy's car. Deal?"
Nod.

"Okay, then. If we take our hands away from your mouth, our time will be spent only on Helen's party, right?"
Nod.

"Okay, Bunny, we're taking our hands away, okay?"

Nod.

The girls put their hands down. Bunny twisted her lips to make sure they still worked.

"I think it's haunted," she said.

"What?"

"The *car*," Bunny said. "Freddy's red-and-yellow heap. I think it's haunted."

"Bunny . . . " Mary Ann sighed.

"I mean it. It's *very* old. I think the ghost of this old man with bad lungs—"

"Bunny, you promised—"

"—coughs in it. And that's why the car jumps like it does—"

"*Bunny!*"

"All right, I'm sorry. Let's talk about the party. I just wanted to tell about the haunting first. Honest. I'm ready now. Let's talk about the party."

Ruthie tested the silence a moment, then cleared her throat. "All right," she said. "We were thinking, maybe we could have it here. I have a big basement and we could have a slumber party down there!"

"But you had a slumber party for *your* birthday, Ruthie," Geraldine reminded her, "just last month."

"But it was fun," Ruthie said.

"Let's do something different this time."

"Well, how about a night party?" Mary Ann suggested. "With boys!"

"Boys! Yuck!" Ruthie said. "Who wants *boys*! All they do is eat and punch each other."

"Let's keep it just us," Geraldine said. "Just us five. It'll be much nicer."

"Well, what can we do that's different?" Mary Ann asked. "All I can think of is a slumber party. Or maybe something after school . . . with supper at someone's house . . ."

"I know!" Bunny cried. "How about a roller skating party! At the rink!"

"Oh! Bunny, that's a great idea!" Ruthie clapped her hands.

"Well, but what will we do, just skate around for a few hours and then go home?" Geraldine asked. "I mean . . . what's the surprise?"

"The surprise is," Bunny began, "that we have a cake ordered that they'll keep for us somewhere at the rink . . . and ice cream and hot dogs and balloons and confetti, and we can have Helen's mom come and her little sister and they can bring all our presents with them, and after about an hour or so of skating we'll all yell 'surprise!' and the people from the rink will bring out the stuff and we'll throw the balloons and the confetti and the streamers and—"

"Hold it!" Geraldine clamped a hand over Bunny's mouth. "I want to talk now, okay, Bunny?"

Bunny nodded and Geraldine took her hand away.

"How can we arrange all that with the rink? Who says they'll do that for us? And what about all the other people there?"

"Helen's birthday is next Thursday," Ruthie said. "There won't be a lot of people skating on a Thursday afternoon, especially if it's a nice warm day like we've been having. We'll tell Helen we're taking her skating for her birthday and the surprise will come when they bring out the cake and confetti and everything. I think it's a good idea, Bun!"

"Maybe . . . " Geraldine admitted. "But how will we get the people at the skating rink to help us pull it off?"

"Leave it to me," Bunny said. "Just leave it to me."

2

"—so anyway, it didn't take us that long to plan the party after we decided to have it at the rink, so I stopped off at the library before I came home. They have these really enormous encyclopedias. Not like ours. I mean, ours is a good set and all, but the ones in the library list just about everybody who was ever born, so you can really—"

"I don't get it," Freddy Junior said, layering butter on a roll. "What do encyclopedias have to do with roller skating?"

"Huh?" Bunny said. "Nothing. It's just that I had the time. And since encyclopedias have something about *everybody*—"

"Not *every*—" Freddy began.

"Almost everybody," Bunny continued, "and I wanted to look up 'Squill' to find the ancestor we had a street named after. Daddy, could you please pass the rolls?"

Her father said, "A street—?" and Bunny went on.

"There must have been *some* ancestor in our family who did something that would get a street named after him, don't you think, Daddy? Don't you think so, too, Mom? What did my great-grandfather do for a living? The one named Squill, I mean?"

Freddy Senior frowned and opened his mouth, but Bunny went right on.

"Because Geraldine is always talking about her great-grandfather, Jeremiah Pennywhistle, who had our street named after him, and I wish I had someone like that I could talk about. Maybe we had an ancestor that fought at the Alamo with Davy Crockett! Do you think we did?"

Her mother opened her mouth, but Bunny went on.

"We studied the Alamo last year. Everybody died there. I mean, all the *Americans* died there, not the Mexicans. Because they won—the Mexicans. But the Americans were all heroes. They were so valiant and brave . . . I know I'd really be proud to—"

"Bunny!"

"What?"

Lucy Squill took a deep breath. "Do—you—want—seconds—on—macaroni!"

"Oh," Bunny replied, "okay, sure. Gee, maybe the man who haunts Freddy's car was famous enough to—"

"Will you quit that stuff about Suzie being haunted?" Freddy Junior said, pointing his fork at his sister.

"Suzie?" his mother asked.

"Marvelle named her. Suzie the Squillmobile. Has a nice ring to it, don't you think?"

"Suzie the Squillmobile," his father muttered to himself.

"Yeah," Freddy Junior sighed. "Marvelle has some neat ideas. Tomorrow we're going to wash Suzie together after school. Get her all shined up and buffed. . . ."

"Can I help, Freddy?" Bunny piped. "Can I? I bet I'm great at washing cars—"

"No."

"—and I'll bet Marvelle would like me to play with John Henry so he won't get in the way while you're washing—"

"The dog will stay in the house while we're washing the car. Forget it, Bunny!" He returned to his macaroni as the phone rang.

"I'll get it," Bunny sang, and reached for the wall telephone. "Hello? . . . Oh, hel-lo, Marvelle!"

Freddy Junior was out of his seat in a flash and moving around to Bunny's side of the table, but Bunny held up her hand.

"Huh?...Oh, sure!...No, I don't mind a bit. I'd love to. Do you want to talk to my brother?... Oh, okay...sure, I'll tell him. 'Bye!" She hung up.

"You hung up on my girlfriend!" Freddy yelled. "She hung up on my girlfriend," he wailed to his parents.

"Your girlfriend didn't want to talk to you," Bunny said. "She called to talk to me. She wants me to play with John Henry tomorrow at her house while you two wash your haunted car." She bit into a cookie. "I said I'd love to. And she said to tell you she'd see you in school. Can I have some more Jell-O, please?"

Freddy Junior stood over his sister and blasted into her ear: "How the heck can you talk every single minute and still manage to eat your entire dinner with second helpings when we're hardly even half-way through ours!"

Bunny shrugged. "I don't know," she said. "I never thought about it."

Later that night, the older Squills prepared for bed.

"How's your headache?" Freddy Senior asked.

"Subsiding," Lucy answered.

"Good. The aspirin helped."

"Yes, and the icepack and the hot compresses . . . "

"And the warm milk . . . "

"And Bunny's bedtime," Lucy finished.

"Ahh, Bunny's bedtime. Silence at last. It was sweet of her to do all the dishes, wasn't it? And fill a nice hot tub for you?"

"Bunny is one of the sweetest people I know," her mother answered. "If she weren't so sweet . . . "

"I know. We'd have outfitted ourselves for ear-plugs years ago. The trouble is, when she's talking, she isn't *listening*. She asks you something and then she won't let you answer! Must drive her teacher crazy."

Lucy smiled.

"What's so funny?" her husband asked.

"I ran into Dora Pinfish at the drugstore. She said Bunny's answers to questions are sometimes longer than the class period."

Freddy Senior groaned.

"It's not that they're wrong answers. It's just that they're a lot more than anyone wants to know!"

"I know, I know . . . "

"Last Saturday I took her shopping for a winter coat. While I was looking in the window of the store, a car pulled up at the curb and the people wanted directions to the country club," Lucy said. "Bunny told them how to get there along with everything they'd pass on the way."

"Everything?" Freddy Senior asked.

"Including the fact that Pennywhistle Lane was named for Jeremiah Pennywhistle, Opata Park's first mayor. And that she, Bunny, was personally acquainted with Geraldine Pennywhistle, the first mayor's great-granddaughter."

"Did those people hang around for the whole speech?" Freddy Senior wanted to know.

"They did. They didn't want to seem impolite, I guess. Anyway, I'm sure they didn't get their directions in the midst of all that chatter. They probably had to stop and ask someone else."

"Bet they wouldn't dare take the chance again." Freddy Senior laughed. "Ah, well... I'm sure Bunny'll outgrow this need to chatter. Someday."

"Someday soon, I hope," his wife yawned.

The next afternoon, Bunny straightened her skirt, pulled in her stomach, and in her best grown-up manner, knocked on the door of the manager's little office at the front of the skating rink.

"Come in," he called.

Bunny opened the door and began talking at the same time.

"Hi," she said. "My name is Bunny Squill. My friends and I want to throw a surprise party for our friend Helen, and we want to have it right here at your skating rink after school. We want to have a cake and hot dogs and streamers and confetti and a whole bunch of helium balloons, and I guess we'll need a big table or something where we can—"

"Wait, wait a minute. . . ." The manager got up from his desk. "Let's slow down a little and you tell me again, okay? You want to have a party here . . . "

"That's right. It's a surprise. We'll bring our friend here and she'll think all we're going to do is skate, but she won't know about all the stuff you'll be holding for us—"

"Holding where?"

"—so after about an hour, the people who work for you will bring out the table with the presents and the—"

"What presents—table—?"

"And we'll all yell 'surprise!' and eat and throw the confetti and—"

"Just a second. What did you say your name was?"

"Don't you have some kind of big table some-where? I guess we could arrange to bring it if you don't—"

"Hey, hey, can I say something here?" the manager asked.

"Huh?"

"Now. What's your name again, first of all. . . . "

"Bunny. Bunny Squill. See, if you don't have a table, then we could have one brought over. Helen's mom has a big station wagon—"

"Well, wait a minute, Bunny . . . I think maybe we could arrange something. . . . Sounds like a good idea . . . " The manager tapped a pencil against his chin.

"Decorations! We'd need some decorations, too, like crepe paper on the walls and maybe one of those big crepe paper balls hanging over the table—"

"Hey! Bunny!"

"Huh?"

"It's okay! Stop talking just a minute. I think we'll be able to help you out. When did you want to have the party?"

But Bunny was looking around the carpeted area at the side of the rink.

"If we had the table over here," she said, "with the streamers coming from here and going right up to the ball hanging *there* . . . "

"Bunny! Hey! When did you want to have the party?"

"Uh—Thursday. Next Thursday. That's Helen's birthday. Look! The table could go right *there.*

Next to that wall. Then it wouldn't be in anyone's way. . . ."

The manager was studying a big book on his desk. He frowned. "Hmmm . . . Friday would be better. Next Thursday the Big Beaver Elementary School is busing over two Girl Scout troops for some after-school skating. How about Friday?"

"Uh-huh," Bunny said absently, "but what about the cake? Should we get it or should you? It should say 'Happy Birthday Helen' and it should have ten candles. Helen's ten. She's younger than all of us, but you'd never know it because she's also taller than—"

"We'll arrange for the cake. And we'll have hot dogs from Sam's down the street. And soda, too. You want soda?"

"Mmmmm. Soda would be good. Oh, no, make that *eleven* candles. There should be one to grow on, right? Only Helen doesn't need to grow any more—she is so tall for someone only nine years old, well, really almost ten. But she's way taller than I am. Wait till you see her. . . ." Bunny walked around the area, pointing and planning while the manager made little notes in his book.

"Okay, Bunny. Cake for Helen . . . eleven candles . . . birthday decorations . . . hot dogs . . . ice cream . . . soda. . . . Did you say ice cream?"

"A big table. There. By the wall."

"Ice cream, right, Bunny?"

"You'll be able to do the decorations? Really? That's great!"

"Listen, Bunny, how many of you will there be?" the manager asked.

"Ice cream, too, okay?" Bunny said, and the manager sighed.

"Yeah. Yeah, ice cream, too. Now how many will there be?"

"Listen," Bunny said, her eyes still wandering over the area. "You won't be sorry about this, honest, because we'll clean everything up afterward so you won't even know we've been here. We'll even take down the decorations and bring a big bag for trash and—"

"Bunny, how many people—"

"—and I promise, if there are other people around skating we won't get in their way at all, because the table will be over there and there'll be only five of us—"

"Five!" the manager said, and wrote it down. "So, that's a birthday party for Helen, ten years old, next Friday after school, five people. . . . "

"Great!" Bunny cried. "That's just great! Wait till I tell the girls. Oh, and maybe you could have some extra hot dogs for Helen's mom and her little sister. . . . "

24

"Well then, that makes it *seven*," the manager said, crossing out numbers in his book. "And who's paying for all this, Bunny?"

"Thanks a lot, Mr.—uh—"

"Hempstetter," the man said. "I'm the manager."

"And don't worry about the money, because each of us is chipping in five dollars of our own money and Helen's mom said she'd make up the difference, but it shouldn't be that much, right, because if you figure around two hot dogs apiece and probably only one for Mary Ann and Helen's little sister—Mary Ann maybe won't even eat any, she hardly eats anything anyway. Oh, and we'll get the confetti, so you don't have to worry about that. So I guess that's all, isn't it. Thanks a million and we'll see you next week, okay, Mr.—uh—"

"Hempstetter," the manager replied, shaking his head. But Bunny was gone.

3

Marvelle Maloney had worked out the arrangement. Freddy Junior would be in charge of the sponges, the buckets, the water and soap, the wax, the scrubbing, and the polishing. Marvelle's job was to walk around the car, peer at it carefully, and point out to Freddy Junior all the parts in which she couldn't see her own reflection. She was also responsible for keeping her dog, John Henry, from jumping up and wrecking the car's shine with his paws until Bunny got there to take him on.

Just as Marvelle leaned over Suzie's right fender to examine her hairdo, John Henry pulled on his leash, yanking Marvelle's wrist.

"Now, John Henry, what's the—oh, I see! It's

Bunny! Here comes Bunny, Freddy! Hi-i, Bunny!"
She waved her arm.

"Goody," Freddy Junior muttered.

"John Henry just lo-oves Bunny-Wunny, don't
you, John Henry?"

The little dog yipped and panted.

"Is it too late to jump in the car and drive away?"
Freddy Junior asked.

"Of course, silly. We're not through washing her
yet. And besides, I asked Bunny to come over and
help, remember?"

"Yeah, I remember. . . . "

"John Henry loves her, don't you, Sweetie-Boo?"
Marvelle picked the little dog up and kissed him on
the nose.

"Aw, don't kiss him," Freddy whined. "Blaghhh!"

Marvelle giggled. "*You* do it," she coaxed, push-
ing the dog at Freddy. "Give Johnsy a little kiss."

"No!"

"Come on, Freddy-Weddy."

"No. Anyway, he hates me, Marvelle. He's already bitten me twice."

"He doesn't hate you. Show him how much you
love him."

"No!"

"Come on, now. . . . Put your face right next to
his nose. . . . "

"Marvelle . . . "

"Freddy, he *loves* you. I just couldn't go out with someone John Henry didn't love, now could I? Just give him a chance to show it. . . . "

Freddy scrunched up his face, squinted his eyes, and put his face near the dog's little black snout.

"Grrrr," John Henry said, showing all the teeth on one side of his mouth.

Freddy stood up quickly just as Bunny reached them. I never thought I'd be this glad to see her, Freddy thought, and out loud he cried, "Hi, Bun!"

"Hi! I just fixed everything up at the skating rink for the party! It's going to be terrific! You looked cute just then, Freddy. Kissing the doggy. Hi, Marvelle! Hi, John Henry!"

Marvelle put the dog down and he ran to Bunny, wagging his tail and panting happily. "Aw, he's so cute," Bunny said. "And he just loves us, doesn't he, Freddy?"

"Loves us," Freddy sighed. He rubbed a gob of wax on Suzie's fender.

"Gee, the car looks pretty," Bunny said, and put her fingers on the red-and-yellow hood.

"Don't touch it!" Freddy Junior barked. Bunny jerked her hand away.

"It looks just like it probably did when it was new," Bunny went on. "And I can see the man who used to own it, sitting there behind the wheel."

Marvelle and Freddy looked at the car.

"You can see Herbie Farnsworth?" Freddy asked.

"No, not Herbie! The man who owned the car *before* him!"

"His father?"

"No, no. *Long* before the Farnsworths." Bunny lowered her voice to a whisper. "The *first* person who owned the car. When it was brand-new, silly!"

Freddy Junior refolded his polishing rag. "Bunny," he said, "when this car was new, you weren't even *born* yet. *I* wasn't even born yet. Now just what the heck are you talking about?"

"Sh!" Bunny peered around. "The first man who owned your car bought it to take his fiancée out riding. Just like you did, Freddy."

"Fiancée! I'm only sixteen," Marvelle said.

"Well, way back then they got married earlier. Anyway, the man who bought this car smoked a lot and he had this terrible cough." Bunny imitated it. "A-*hah*, a-*hah*, a-*hah*!" she coughed. "Like that."

Freddy gave the car a final swipe with the rag. "Knock it off, will you, Bunny—"

"A-*hah*!" Bunny finished. "See, the man who owned this car had this *ter*-rible, *aw*-ful, *pain*-ful smoker's cough, and now he still sits behind the wheel and haunts the car and coughs and coughs and coughs whenever the motor runs—"

"Now, just bag it, Bunny!" Freddy Junior yelled and stamped his foot, kicking over a bucket of soapy water. "Just quit blabbering for a minute! Number one, Suzie isn't *that* old. The first guy who owned her is probably alive and well and driving his Ferrari to the racetrack or something! And number two, even if he isn't, Bunny, Suzie coughs because the accelerator pump isn't squirting the gas in fast enough, like I've told you about a hundred and one times, Bunny, so just *quit* making stuff up so you can have something to *say*, okay?"

Bunny frowned. "I'm not," she said. "I really can see the poor man behind the—"

"Marvelle and I are going to the movies," Freddy said.

"We are?" Marvelle asked. "In the afternoon?"

Freddy grabbed John Henry's leash from Marvelle's wrist. "So here, Bunny, take John Henry and walk him around the block a few thousand times. And then just let him in the back door. Got that? 'Bye, Bunny!" He reached for the car door and pushed Marvelle into the front seat.

" 'Bye, Bunny," Marvelle said over her shoulder.

"A-*hah*, a-*hah*, a-*hah*," the car said, as Freddy turned on the ignition and stepped on the gas.

" 'Bye," Bunny said as John Henry licked her fingers.

That night when Freddy Senior pulled into the driveway, Bunny was ready for him. She was standing in the open doorway as he came up the walk carrying his briefcase full of work.

"Daddy! Wait till you hear what I did!"

Her father kissed her on the cheek and stepped into the hall.

"Just hold it a minute, Bunny," he said, "while I tell the family—"

"I fixed the whole thing at the skating rink. I talked to the manager and all we girls have to do is get Helen to the rink with our skates and the manager will have all the—"

"Hold it, Bunny!" Freddy Senior said loudly. Bunny held it because her father hardly ever said anything loudly. "I want the whole family in the living room. Where's your mother?"

"In the kitchen."

"And Freddy Junior?"

"In his room . . ."

"Go get them, will you please?" her father asked. "And bring them in here?"

"*Mom!*" Bunny yelled. "*Freddy! Come out here into the living room! Daddy wants you!*"

Freddy Senior winced. "Bunny, if I'd wanted yelling, *I* could have yelled, you know," he said.

"Sorry," Bunny said. "It's easier."

Lucy and Freddy Junior scurried into the room.

"What is it?" Lucy asked. "Is anything wrong?"

"Better be good, Dad," Freddy said. "I was having a very important phone conversation."

" 'I love your beautiful hair, Mar-velle,' " Bunny sang at him. " 'And I love your beautiful ee-yyy-es!' "

Her brother glared at her.

"Nothing's wrong," Freddy Senior said, holding up his hands. "I just have some big news. Well, actually, nothing definite yet, but it *could* be big news."

"What is it, dear?" Lucy asked.

"Well! How would you all like to live in *London*?"

"*London*?" Freddy Junior squeaked. "You mean England?"

"That's where it was last time I checked," his father answered.

"London?" Lucy repeated.

Bunny, for once, was speechless.

"London," Freddy Senior repeated, and turned to his wife. "Harvey just called me into his office and told me about it." Harvey Burnside was Mr. Squill's boss at the Burnside & Burnside advertising agency.

"Well, tell us!" Lucy exclaimed. "Tell us about it!"

Freddy Junior slumped to the couch.

"Okay," his father said, and took a deep breath. "Now, remember, this is only in the talking stage. There's nothing definite, understand?"

"Go on," his wife said.

"Well, Harvey's been working on getting this English toffee account. These people want to see their English toffee over here—"

"What's toffee?" Bunny asked.

"Candy. A kind of chewy candy."

"Oh, I *love* chewy candy!" Bunny cried.

"Yes. Well, the English company hopes other Americans will love it, too. Anyway, you know what a sportsman Harvey is—"

"Yes, we know," Lucy interrupted. "He's got you out there playing golf practically every weekend and tennis and handball—"

"Right. And that reminds me, he's supposed to call about a golf date he's set up with these English representatives who're coming over. He met the president of this English toffee company on his golfing vacation this past July and they got talking. This guy is a big golfer, too. And that's how we may end up with this account!"

Lucy kissed his cheek. "That's wonderful, dear," she said. "But why would we all have to go and live in London? That is, if they're selling their toffee over *here*."

"Maybe they want us to taste it," Bunny said. "Maybe they want us there as representatives. To eat their toffee all the time and see how good it is, so Daddy can sell it better. Maybe our family will be the Official Toffee-Eating—"

"Bunny," her mother said, and Bunny closed her mouth. "Go on, Freddy."

"All right. What Harvey has in mind is this: If Burnside & Burnside gets the account—and it is a big one—then someone from the firm would have to go over to England and get things rolling."

"And that someone would be you, Daddy!" Bunny cried.

"Right. And then, that someone would stay there for about a year to solicit other English businesses for the firm."

"A year?" Freddy Junior whined from the couch.

"A year. Harvey would give us a year to see if we could pick up some more accounts. And maybe he'd start a branch over there."

"But you haven't got the toffee account yet, though," Lucy said.

"That's right, we don't. So it's all just in the talking stage for now. But it is a possibility. Harvey just told me about it and I wanted to tell you."

"Wow!" Bunny squealed.

"Wow," her mother whispered.

"Oh, wo-ow," Freddy Junior groaned.

"Just remember, it's only a possibility," Freddy Senior said again. "It may not happen."

"But it may!" Bunny cried.

"Da-ad," Freddy Junior said, and his voice cracked.

"Oh, boy," Bunny sighed. "We move to London. The Queen lives there! And Prince Charles! And Princess Diana! And they all live in beautiful castles that you can roam around in, and never find anyone else in your family for days and days! And in London they say 'fah-ster' instead of 'faster' and..."

"Da-ad!" Freddy Junior croaked again.

"What *is* it, son?"

"Well, it's just that... I mean... Dad, you don't understand. If you go to London, I have to stay here."

"What?"

"I have to stay, Dad. Look, I'll take care of the house while you're gone, okay?"

"Freddy, don't be silly. You can't stay here," his mother said.

"I *have* to. Look, Mom, I'll water all the plants."

"Freddy—"

"You don't *understand!*" Freddy wailed again. "If I go to London, Marvelle will find another boyfriend just like"—he snapped his fingers—"that!"

"Now, Freddy, if we move to England for a year, you move with us," his mother said firmly.

"Do you know how long it took me to get the courage to ask her out?" Freddy cried. "And now, just when we're—I mean, just when . . . Aww, Dad, can't you say no?"

"Freddy . . . ," his father began.

"English girls are nice, too," Bunny said. "And they talk better than you."

"Bunny," her mother warned. "Now, Freddy, just think of all the opportunities—the wonderful opportunities of living, actually living in another country for a year!"

"Oh, boo-oy!" Freddy wailed.

"Now what?"

"The cars!"

"The what?"

"The *cars!*" Freddy moaned. "I just learned how to drive on the *right* side of the road. Over *there*, they drive on the *left* side! And Suzie's *wheel* will have to be moved! And how do we ship Suzie over there anyway?"

"Now, look, Freddy," his mother said, putting a hand on his shoulder. "Let's not worry about any of those things. Your dad just said nothing's definite yet anyway. We'll have to wait and see what happens. Now, let's all go wash up for dinner. Bunny?"

" 'Fah-ster,' " Bunny said. " 'Fah-ster' and 'mahster' and 'to-*mah*-to.' "

"What?" Lucy said. "Bunny, what are you saying?"

"I'm talking 'English,' " Bunny answered. "And here's how you hold your teacup." She held an imaginary cup with her pinkie sticking out. "This is the way they do it. Every day at four o clock. Every sing-le day. They pour tea and eat little rolls and—"

"Bunny!" the others yelled.

"Huh?"

Her father took Bunny by the shoulders and knelt to face her.

"Now look, Bunny," he said, "this news has to stay within the family, understand? Don't talk about it until it's set. Because otherwise I'd look pretty silly, wouldn't I? If it doesn't come off, I mean. So this is our family secret for now until I get the word. Okay?"

"Sure, Daddy."

"And you, too, Freddy. Not a word to Marvelle or anyone yet. Agreed?"

"Not even to Marv-elle?" Freddy groaned. "Even if I say nothing's definite?"

"Not a word," Bunny said, looking up at her brother. "You'll just have to learn to keep your mouth shut, Freddy."

The other three Squills burst out laughing.

"What'd I say?" Bunny asked.

On the following Thursday, the day of Helen's birthday, the four friends approached Helen at her locker one minute after the end of school. Bunny's face was flushed with excitement.

"Ready, girls?" Geraldine said and held up her hand. "One . . . two . . . *three!*"

"Hap-py birth-day to you," they sang. "Hap-py birth-day to you. Hap-py birth-day dear Hel-en! Hap-py birth-day to you-ooo!"

Helen banged her locker door shut.

"Gee . . . thanks!" she said with a smile. "I thought you all forgot. No one said a thing all day—"

"We didn't forget," Mary Ann told her. "We just

wanted to surprise you! Now you have to come with us."

"Where?"

"You'll see . . . " Ruthie said.

"First we have to go to my locker, though," Bunny said. "Come on, Helen!"

Helen, pleased and confused, began to follow them down the hall. "My birthday presents are in your locker," she said to Bunny.

"No . . . " Bunny giggled.

"You'll see!" Ruthie said again.

Bunny opened her locker door, and with a clatter and crash, five pairs of roller skates fell out onto the floor.

"Gee, Bunny, you could've hung them," Geraldine complained.

"Roller skates?" Helen said. "Hey—that pair is mine."

"Right!" Bunny said. "I picked them up at your house this morning after you left for school. Your mother had them waiting."

"My mother? What's going on?" Helen asked.

"We're taking you skating for your birthday," Mary Ann explained. "And we have to get over to the rink right now."

"Skating? Oh, that sounds like fun," Helen said. "Different, anyway . . . a skating party after school . . . "

"Oh, but that's not all—" Bunny said, and Geraldine clapped a hand over her mouth.

"Come on, Helen," she said, still holding Bunny. "Girls, grab your own skates and let's go." As they walked, she hissed in Bunny's ear: "It's a *surprise*, Squill, remember? Now *sh!*"

"What's that?" Mary Ann asked as they arrived at the rink.

"It's a school bus. What does it look like?" Geraldine said. "Bunny, what's a school bus doing here? I thought you said the place would be practically ours!"

"I wonder if the school buses in London are double-decker?" Bunny asked thoughtfully.

"Who cares!" Ruthie cried, and pointed. "Look at that! About twenty thousand Girl Scouts are getting off that bus! Hey, Bunny—"

"Let's go inside," Bunny said. "Let's see what the inside looks like."

The inside of the roller skating rink looked exactly as it had when Bunny made the arrangements with Mr. Hempstetter, the manager. No streamers, no crepe paper ball, no table on the side.

"Helen, would you mind waiting over there for a second?" Ruthie asked sweetly, but her voice cracked. Helen shrugged and stepped over to the candy machines. "Now, Bunny!" Ruthie whispered harshly. "Where are the decorations? Where's the table? Where's all the stuff you said would be here when *we* got here?"

"Yeah, Bunny," Mary Ann said. "What's going on, anyway?"

" 'Leave it to me,' Bunny," Geraldine growled. "That's what you said. Well, we left it to you and *now* what?"

"Just—just wait a second," Bunny told them. "Just stay right there. . . . " She held up a calming hand, though she was feeling far from calm, and inched her way over to the manager's office. He was just coming out of it.

"Mr.—uh—"

"Hempstetter," he said. "Bunny, right? The talker? What are you doing here today?"

"It's Helen's party day, that's what I'm doing here, Mr. Handstepper. Look!" She pointed. "That's Helen, standing right over there. And those other three—they are Ruthie, Geraldine, and Mary Ann. And they're all mad. Where are the—"

"Now, hold it, Bunny, you're down for tomorrow, remember?" Mr. Hempstetter said.

"—decorations you promised? And the table! I told you Thursday was Helen's birthday—"

"Sure, you told me, Bunny. And I told *you* that the Girl Scouts from Big Beaver were coming Thursday. And I put you down for Friday and you said okay."

"What?"

"Look, Bunny, I'm sorry." Mr. Hempstetter shrugged. "Come on into the office if you want to check the book. And then come back tomorrow—you and your friends—and everything will be just the way you wanted it."

"No, it won't," Bunny sighed. "It was supposed to be a surprise. A surprise party for Helen. Besides, *today's* her birthday, not tomorrow. . . ."

Mr. Hempstetter shrugged again. "Sorry," he repeated, and went to look after the Big Beaver Girl Scouts.

"I wonder if they have Girl Scouts in London," Bunny grumbled, and turned to walk back to her friends.

Geraldine was tapping her foot and glowering.

"*Well?*" she snapped. "Well, Bunny?"

"Uh, he—"

"He *what?*" Mary Ann demanded.

"He has us down for tomorrow. Everything's set to go for tomorrow, just the way we—"

"Tomorrow!" Ruthie shrieked.

"It was just a—I just—the Girl Scouts—" Bunny stammered.

"May I come back now?" Helen called to them. "Are we going skating?"

"Great," Geraldine mumbled. "Just great."

"What will we do?" Mary Ann wanted to know. "Should we tell her? Should we come back tomorrow or what?"

Just then the door of the rink burst open.

"Hi! Surprise!" Helen's little sister called and everyone turned to look at her, including the Girl Scouts. "Happy birthday, Helen! Mom's right behind me with all the presents! Gee, what's the matter with everybody, anyway?"

"I didn't think it was *that* bad," Bunny said to her mother that evening. "I mean, we did go skating and that was fun, and Helen did get all our presents and she liked them, so that part was okay...."

"But you didn't have any of the festivities," her mother said. "Or a birthday cake. Right?"

"Well..."

"Because you didn't hear the man when he said he couldn't do the party on Thursday, isn't that right?"

"Well..."

"And, Bunny, why didn't you hear the man when he told you Friday instead of Thursday?"

"I guess I wasn't paying attention," Bunny said.

"I know it was my fault, Mom. I was so excited about Helen's party and how we were going to surprise her that I just didn't pay attention to the part about the Girl Scouts. I was picturing the whole thing in my mind: how we'd get it all—"

"Bunny . . ."

"—together and how we'd tell her . . . I was picturing how the place would look when it was—"

"Bunny—"

"—decorated. . . . I even had the colors picked out. The crepe paper would be green and yellow and the—"

"Bunny!"

"What?"

"That's what you did with the manager of the skating rink, isn't it?"

"What's what I did?"

"You talked so much, you didn't hear what he had to say back. Bunny, you do it all the time. Wednesday I asked you to bring that pile of clothes to the dry cleaner's after school and there it is, still sitting on the chair. Because you were so busy talking about how Marvelle Maloney's dog was probably a brand-new breed instead of the scruffy mutt that he is."

"He's not a scruffy mutt, Mom!"

"He's cute, Bunny, but he's still a scruffy mutt. And that's beside the point! Sometimes, Bunny, you have to *listen* as well as talk. Did you hear me?"

"Aw, just because he's got a little scraggly beard doesn't mean he's scruffy. . . . And I still think maybe there's some new breed that—"

"Bunny! I was trying to tell you something about listening and you're not listening!"

"I'm listening," Bunny said, looking up into her mother's face. "What did you say?"

5

On weekday mornings, the Squills made their own breakfasts, bumping into each other as they reached for pans, bowls, silverware, and range buttons. The morning after Bunny's big flop at the skating rink, Freddy Junior was late coming down to the kitchen.

"Where's Freddy?" his mother asked. She was wearing her oldest clothes: cotton pants with paint stains on them and one of her husband's ripped shirts.

"He's still upstairs," Bunny answered. "Why are you dressed like that, Mom? Is it costume day at the nursery school?"

"No. Fingerpainting day. If that boy doesn't come down soon, he'll be late."

"Pahss the milk, please, Fah-ther," Bunny said.

Freddy Senior handed her the carton. "Don't talk that way in front of your friends, Bunny," he said. "Remember—"

"I know, I know. Nothing's definite. Pahss the mah-gerine, please."

At that point, Freddy Junior clumped into the room. "Knock it off, Bunny," he growled. "You sound weird anyhow."

"I'm just practicing," Bunny told him. "By the time we get there I'll sound just like an English person. Listen to this." She dropped her jaw straight down. "How—now, brown cow—"

"Stuff it, Bunny!"

Lucy patted her son's arm. "Now, Freddy, don't talk that way to your sister. What are you having for breakfast?"

"Nothing."

"You have to have something," Bunny said. "Breakfast is the most important meal of the day. In London, they have great big—"

"Bunny—" Freddy raised his arm and Bunny ducked.

"Stop it, Freddy. Stop it, Bunny," Lucy warned. "The day hasn't even started yet and I've got a head-ache. Bunny, you keep London on the back burner. Freddy, you stop moping until we find out one way or another what we're doing."

"Maybe Marvelle could visit us in our flat," Bunny said, and the other three Squills yelled, "*Bunny!*"

"Just trying to be helpful," she said.

As they began to file out of the house, Bunny said, "Freddy? Can I have a ride to school?"

"No!"

"It's not out of your way if you cut through—"

"No!"

"—Abner Lane and take Elm Street to Rivermont and—"

"No!"

"—pick up Marvelle first. Please? I want to hear the old man cough—"

"No!" Freddy jumped into his car without opening the door. Bunny stood next to it while it sputtered and wheezed and she shook her head sadly. "Poor man," she said, as Freddy made a face and backed Suzie down the driveway.

"The poor old man has such a cough," Bunny sang as she made her own way down the driveway. "Even when the mo-tor's off. . . . " She looked up and down the street. Sure enough, there was Geraldine Pennywhistle, waving good-bye to her father as they both left their house.

"Hi, Geraldine!" Bunny called. "Let's walk to school together. Freddy wanted to give us a ride, but it's such a beautiful day I said we'd walk. Isn't it a beautiful day? Geraldine?"

Geraldine continued to walk by as if she hadn't heard.

"Hey!" Bunny said, starting to run. "Geraldine! I'm talking to you!" But Geraldine kept walking with her eyes straight ahead, even as Bunny caught up to her.

"Gee, Geraldine, did something happen to your hearing?" she asked. "Do you have cotton in your ears? Did you have an earache last night and your mom put that gooey stuff in your ears that runs all down your neck and oils up your pajamas? That happened to me once and I could hardly hear anything for—"

"*No*, Bunny," Geraldine said, turning to her for the first time. "I can hear you just fine, but I don't want to. You and your talk-talk-talk just ruined everything yesterday, and I'm mad at you. Okay? I'm really mad. So go walk to school by yourself!"

"But—we can still go back to the rink today," Bunny said. "And the manager will put up all the stuff. . . and we can have the cake and all . . . "

"It's not the same, Bunny! Now go on! Walk! Shoo, Squill!"

Bunny stopped. "Well!" she said. "I don't think you're being very nice about it at all, Geraldine. I mean, after all, *anyone* can make a mistake. Didn't *you* ever make a mistake? Geraldine?"

Geraldine was already at the end of the block.

"Well, okay for you," Bunny called after her. "Just for that, I won't tell you about—" Suddenly she clapped her own hand over her mouth. Ooh, I nearly said "London," she realized. And after all Daddy told us about not mentioning it! Well, she thought, I wouldn't tell Geraldine even if I could The big snob!

But Mary Ann and Ruthie didn't seem angry at Bunny that day. And Helen even stopped by her locker to thank her for thinking of the surprise and getting her skates. So Bunny was feeling a little better as she skipped home after school. Besides, tomorrow was Saturday, and Saturdays were the best days of all.

When Bunny arrived home, she found her father in the living room. He was wearing his khaki pants and a striped casual shirt.

"Hi, Daddy! What are you doing home so early?"

Freddy Senior smiled at her. "Don't you remember? I told you I was playing golf this afternoon. I need some practice for my foursome tomorrow morning." He opened the closet door and pulled out his bag of clubs. "I've got to get my game in shape for that upcoming date with the men from Peterson's Olde English Toffee."

"Peterson's Olde English Toffee? Is that the name of the company we're going to work for?"

"*Maybe* going to work for. And yes, that's it. Tell Mom I'll be back in time for supper." He swung the bag over his shoulder.

"Okay. Is Freddy at Marvelle's?"

"I guess so. I haven't seen him."

"Maybe I'll go over there and talk to them," Bunny said.

"No, Bunny. Leave Freddy and Marvelle alone. Why don't you stay here and read some of these books I brought home about London." He pointed to the coffee table where a stack of books and brochures rested next to a picture of Bunny as a baby with her mouth open.

"Ohh!" Bunny breathed. "That's a good idea. I'll learn where everything is and then I'll know where to go and what to see and what to order in the restaurants and what to—"

" 'Bye, Bun," her father called.

Freddy Junior was up and out of the house early Saturday morning. Marvelle and her parents were spending the day in Wakefield at Marvelle's grandparents' house and Freddy Junior had grudgingly promised to pick up John Henry before they left.

"He won't go with me," Freddy had complained to Marvelle. "He hates me."

"He loves you," Marvelle insisted. "And he loves to ride in Suzie."

"He *hates* to ride in Suzie," Freddy moaned. "He gets carsick!"

"He only got sick once," Marvelle told him, "because you fed him hot dogs before the ride."

"I fed him hot dogs because he jumped as high as my shoulder to grab them out of my hand!" Freddy complained. But in the end, he agreed to mind John Henry for the whole day. "The things I do for love," he mumbled, slamming Suzie's door and driving off toward Rivermont Road.

Bunny was sitting at the breakfast table when her mother came in.

"Did I just hear Suzie pulling away?" Lucy asked.

"Uh-huh," Bunny answered around a mouthful of toast. "Freddy went to get John Henry. He's baby-sitting for him today."

"Really?" Lucy poured orange juice for herself and more for Bunny. "I thought he hated that dog."

"He does. It's mutual. But he doesn't hate Marvelle. And Marvelle asked him to."

"Oh. Well, I'm going shopping, Bunny. Do you want to come?"

"Mmm, no. No, thanks, Mom. I'm going to stay

here and finish looking at all this stuff about England Daddy brought home." She peered down at a pamphlet on the table in front of her.

"Well . . . okay, but you'll be by yourself for a while. Daddy's playing golf and I'm not sure when your brother or I will be back. . . ."

"I don't mind."

"Why don't you call Geraldine?"

Bunny sniffed. "Geraldine is a snob," she said.

"Mmm. Well, so's her mother. But if you get them off the subject of the town history, they can be nice. I thought you were friendly with Geraldine."

"I was. But she's mad over what happened with Helen's party."

"Ah. Well, I hope you learned something from that experience, Bunny."

Bunny looked down at her pamphlet.

"Hey, Mom? Did you know that Henry the Eighth chopped off two of his wives' heads?"

"Bunny—"

"I mean, he didn't chop them off himself, personally, but he—"

"Bunny?"

"Huh?"

"I'm going. Take phone messages."

"I will."

It was a sunny morning. Bunny took her stackful of books and brochures into the room that her father called "the den," her mother called "the TV room," and her brother called "the rock room," because that's where the stereo was. Bunny herself had always called it "the playroom." Now she spread her things around her on the floor and picked them up one at a time. " 'Tour Number One,' " she read out loud. " 'The West End and Buckingham Palace. You see: London's theaters, Trafalgar Square, Pall Mall, Piccadilly Circus'—Oh, boy, they take you to a circus, too! And 'Regent Street and Oxford Street and—' "

The phone rang.

" '—and Marble Arch and Hyde Park and—' "

The phone rang again. Bunny got to her feet, still reading.

" 'Big Ben, Whitehall, the Mall, and St. James's Palace!' Ooooh!" She picked up the receiver. "Hello?"

"Hello, there," the voice said. "Lucy?"

"No, this is Bunny. Mom's not here. May I take a message? 'The Changing of the Guard'! Wow! I always wanted to see the Changing of the Guard!"

"Bunny? Hello?"

"Hello. Who's this?"

"It's Mr. Burnside, Bunny. Harvey Burnside. Is your dad home?"

"They change the guard at Buckingham Palace! I remember!"

"*Bunny!*" Mr. Burnside yelled into the phone. "*Is your dad home?* I think we have a bad connection!"

"No, Daddy's not home, Mr. Burnside. Should I have him call you? Oooh," she said, turning a page of her booklet. "St. Paul's Cathedral is beau-tiful."

"He can't call me, Bunny," Mr. Burnside said, still yelling into the phone. "I'm calling from the airport. I'm going duck-hunting for a week in Canada with a client. Your father knows—"

"Oh, my gosh! The Tower of London!" Bunny cried. "That's where two Mrs. Henry the Eighths had their heads cut off! Did you know about that, Mr. Burnside? About those Mrs. Eighths?"

"Bunny, listen carefully now. I want you to give your dad an important message, okay?"

"He told us, Mr. Burnside! He told us about England—"

"Yes, well, that's what this is about, Bunny. Tell Freddy that it's a go on that date we were talking about yesterday."

"—and Fleet Street is supposed to be—huh? Did you say it's a *go?*"

"Right. Tell him McBundy's excited about it. That's McBundy—from Peterson's. He hears your dad's terrific."

"He is! He is terrific!"

"Well, tell him to practice and get even better. The date's set for the fourth of next month, so that doesn't give him much time. It's a Saturday, so that'll be a busy day at the—"

"The *fourth*! October *fourth*? But that's only two weeks away!"

"—busy day at the club, so he'd better book us in there right away."

"Book us right away! For the fourth! Oh, boy, I just can't believe it!" Bunny shouted. "The Changing of the Guard—"

"Tell Freddy we're counting on him, and I'll see him in a week. Oh, listen, they're calling my plane. Got to run. Thanks, Bunny. So long!"

"—and the Tower of London, here we come! Gosh, that sure happened fast, Mr. Burnside! Daddy only told us last week that it was even a possibility! And now it's really happening! Does the Piccadilly Circus have trapeze artists, Mr. Burnside? Mr. Burnside?" Bunny stared at the receiver. "Gee, he hung up. And here I am all alone with this big news!" She dropped her pamphlet to the floor. "How can I sit here and wait till everyone comes back?" She began to pace. "The golf course is too far for me to walk . . . I don't know which store Mom is in . . . Freddy could be just about anywhere

56

with John Henry. . . . We're going to London!" She screamed at the ceiling. "It's a *go!* We're moving to London! England!"

6

Bunny kept all her dolls and stuffed animals on her bed, spread out in a row against the wall, with one special doll on her pillow. She rotated the dolls so that each got a turn to spend the day at the end of the bed. Now she raced to tell them all that they would soon be on a new bed in a new house in a new country.

Today's doll-on-the-pillow was Brenda, the stuffed giraffe. Bunny picked it up and screamed, "Brenda! You're going on an airplane! A big jet airplane! You're going to sit on my bed in England! And you won't be a giraffe anymore, you'll be a gir-ahffe!"

Excitedly, she reported the details to each toy,

including the sights on the tours she had read about in her pamphlets. But telling the toys wasn't enough. She needed real live people to talk to. Real live people wouldn't just stare back at her as her toys did. Real live people would react, would respond, would be just as excited and enthusiastic as Bunny herself was.

"I'll call Ruthie!" Bunny cried out loud. And then she said, "No, I can't. Daddy said not to tell anyone. Oh, but wait! He said not to tell anyone because nothing was definite. But now it is! Now it's definite! So I can tell . . . *everybody!*" She raced downstairs for the phone.

Ruthie's line was busy. Bunny slammed down the receiver impatiently. I can't wait, she thought. I can't wait for Ruthie to hang up. I'll run over there right now! I'll run to Helen's and to Mary Ann's and to—

Geraldine's!

Geraldine Pennywhistle.

Bunny pursed her lips. Miss Perfect Pennywhistle, who never makes mistakes! Having a silly old street named after your great-grandfather is nothing compared to moving to London, England, where the Queen lives! Talk about ancestors!

Bunny pulled on a sweatshirt over her jeans and T-shirt and raced out of the house.

"I know you're mad at me, Geraldine," she began

quickly when Geraldine answered her knock, "but I wanted to say that you won't have Bunny Squill to kick around anymore, because I'm leaving town."

Geraldine tilted her head and frowned. "You mean you're running away?" she asked. "Just because I got mad at you?"

"Oh, sure, Geraldine, sure. Of course I'm not running away. I'm moving. We're all moving. My family, that is. We're moving away."

"Come on, Bunny, if this a way to get me to feel sorry for you and quit being mad because you did such a dumb—"

"Feel *sorry!*" Bunny exclaimed. "Feel *sorry* because I'm going to live in London, England, and have tea with the Queen and Princess Diana?"

"Bunny, what are you talking about, anyway?" Geraldine asked with a sigh as she leaned against her doorjamb.

"Geraldine," Bunny said, "this is the last chance you'll have to say good-bye and good luck to someone who's on her way to Buckingham Palace. And I'm not kidding, either. So good-bye. And just to show you there's no hard feelings, good luck to you, too!" She turned to march down the Pennywhistles' steps.

"Wait a minute," Geraldine called. "Is this on the level, Squill? Are you really moving? To *England*?

Because I just said hi to your mother this morning as she was leaving your house, and she sure didn't say anything about moving to England or anything. All she said was her sneakers finally split a seam."

"She didn't *know*," Bunny answered over her shoulder. "The call from my father's boss just came through. I was the only one home. So good-bye, Geraldine. I hope someday you get over being mad."

Bunny ran to Ruthie's next.

"*Lon*-don?" Ruthie squealed. "Oh, wow, Bunny! I just can't believe it! When are you leaving?"

"Two weeks," Bunny said. "I can't stay long—I have to go home and pack. But I wanted to tell you now because you're one of my very best friends."

"Wow, Bunny," Ruthie said again. "But isn't two weeks a little sudden?"

"Yes," Bunny nodded. "But that's what Mr. Burnside said. He was going away on a trip and he wanted my dad to know now so he could get ready. It's so exciting, I mean, I've been reading all about it— the castles, the museums, all that stuff—but I still don't know what you're supposed to wear when you visit the Queen."

"You're visiting the Queen?"

Bunny nodded. "Sure. Important Americans always visit the Queen. And this man in England—

the president of this company we're going to work for—he says my dad's terrific!"

"Golly..."

"So," Bunny shrugged, "it just stands to reason we'll be visiting the Queen. The thing that I'm the most excited about, though, is seeing Princess Diana up close!"

"Gol-*ly!*"

"But I'll take my Polaroid with me and send you a picture of us together, okay?"

"Gee, Bunny, won't you be going to school, though? I mean, until you leave?"

"I don't know, Ruthie. Probably I'll be too busy shopping and packing. But maybe we'll see each other before I go." She waved and began to run all the way to Helen's.

By the time Bunny got home from her friends' houses, her mother had arrived with her new pair of running shoes and seven bags of groceries. She was unloading them from the back of the family station wagon as Bunny ran up to her.

"Mom! Oh, Mom—"

"Bunny, just wait before you start talking and grab some of these packages for me."

"But, Mom—!"

"No—" Lucy held up her hand. "I don't want to hear a thing until every one of those bags is on the kitchen table."

"But—"

"Here!" Lucy pushed a bulging brown shopping bag into Bunny's arms.

"All right," Bunny said, from behind a protruding box of Shredded Wheat, "but you're not going to need all of this stuff." She turned and marched toward the door.

"What?" her mother said.

"You're not going to need this stuff!" Bunny repeated. "It's all going to be wasted. We'll be on a plane before even half of it's gone!"

"A plane," Lucy sighed, "right." She cradled a brown bag in each arm as she followed her daughter through the side door.

"Come on, Bunny," she said. "Four more bags to go."

"I mean it, Mom. We'll be eating fish and chips long before you get to defrost all this meat you bought. . . ."

"Now, Bunny, your father and I warned you about discussing this England thing before—"

"But that's just *it*, Mom! Mr. Burnside called this morning. He said it's a *go!*"

"*What?*"

" 'Tell your father it's a *go!*' For October fourth."

"October *fourth*? But that's two weeks from now!"

"That's what *I* said. But Mr. Burnside said that Mr. Mac—McBundy—hears Daddy is terrific. And he's really excited about it. And that Daddy should book everything now."

Lucy let the bags she was holding slide onto a kitchen chair.

"Now, wait a minute, Bunny," she said. "I'd better call Harvey Burnside to get this all straight."

"You can't," Bunny said, beginning to jump up and down. "You can't call him. He's going hunting or something. He was at the airport. He said it was very important for me to tell Daddy that it's a go and that Daddy should book us all for the fourth of October! He said it was *very important!*"

Lucy sank into the chair herself, squashing a shopping bag.

"This is unreal," she said. "I just can't believe this . . . "

"I know! Isn't it wonderful? Mom, did you know that kings and queens have had their coronations in Westminster Abbey for over *seven hundred years*? And that a lot of them are even *buried* in there?"

"Bunny—"

"And there's a clock, it has a name, it's called Big Bill—"

"Ben."

"Ben?"

"Bunny!"

"What?"

"Stop talking for just a minute, okay? Let me think. . . ."

"Sure, Mom. You think. Mom, do you know that game we used to play when I was little? 'London Bridge Is Falling Down'? Well, it isn't! I mean, it didn't! I mean, you can cross over London Bridge today! The real—"

"Bunny, go get the rest of the groceries and do it right now!" her mother commanded and then as Bunny ran to obey, she sat staring at the kitchen wallpaper and its bright print of yellow daisies.

The front door banged open.

"I'm home!" Freddy Junior yelled. "With this mutt! Ow!"

"Go help your sister bring the groceries in," Lucy called weakly from the kitchen.

"I will if you can get this—ow!—mutt's teeth out of the leg of my jeans—"

His mother came into the living room. She knelt to pat John Henry, who immediately let go of Freddy Junior's pants and began to lick her hand. She picked the dog up and stood in the open doorway, watching her children at the car.

"Yap," John Henry barked and licked her face. She began to relax until she heard:

"You're *crazy!*"

"I'm not. We're leaving next week!"

"You're *crazy!*"

"Nope. I talked to Mr. Burnside myself this morning."

"You're *crazy!*"

"Will you stop saying that, Freddy?" You're just being stubborn, that's all. We're really going. Ask Mom."

"Mo-om!" Freddy wailed from the driveway, though his mother was standing right at the door. "Hey, Mo-om!"

"Freddy, be quiet," she said, and John Henry growled at him. "And listen, I got it from Bunny, same as you. But she mentioned the man's name— the one from the toffee company—and she told us the date that Mr. Burnside said. Now, Bunny talks a lot but I don't think she could have made up those things."

"Well, thanks!" Bunny said indignantly.

"I'm sorry, Bunny," her mother said, "but this isn't just idle chatter. What you told us is that our whole lives are going to be uprooted. So if this is some sort of game or wishful thinking or anything like that, you'd better say so now, before I put the house on the market."

Bunny placed one hand over her heart and raised the other. "I-swear-I'm-telling-you-exactly-what-Mr.-Burnside-told-me-to-tell-Daddy-this-morning-on-the-phone," she intoned. "And may lightning strike me dead, if—"

"All right, Bunny, that's enough. We don't have to go that far. Now you both get these groceries in the house and unpack them. Put them away, too."

"What are you going to do, Mom?" Bunny asked.

"I'm going over to the golf course to get your father. There seems to be something wrong that he's the last to hear about this—"

"Hi, Lucy!" a woman from down the street called. It was Bitsy Pennywhistle, Geraldine's mother. "Congratulations! Send me some Harris tweeds! I know a divine place on Regent Street."

Lucy glared at her daughter. "Bunny . . . ," she growled.

Freddy Senior arrived home in the station wagon with his wife. His face was red and perspiring. He took Bunny by herself into the den-TV-rock-play-room and closed the door. Then he sat down on a footstool and pulled Bunny toward him so that their eyes were on the same level.

"All right, Bunny," he said. "I want you to tell me exactly what Mr. Burnside said to you on the phone this morning. And I want it in exact quotes, understand?"

"Uh-huh."

"I mean, you don't elaborate, you don't exaggerate, you don't punctuate, you just reiterate."

"Great," Bunny sighed. "Okay." She told him what she said and what she heard. When she finished, her father took his hands from her waist and blew out his breath.

"Well," he said, "so this is it."

"This is it," Bunny repeated.

"But the fourth! So soon! I mean, I thought I'd get to meet the people involved. There were to be a few golf dates, some lunches . . . at least that's what I thought. . . . These things usually happen over a period of time. . . . "

"Mr. Mac—"

"McBundy."

"Right. Mr. Burnside said Mr. McBundy heard you were terrific," Bunny said again.

"That's nice, but I would have thought he'd want to find that out for himself."

"He will," Bunny said, "on the fourth."

The four Squills spent the rest of Saturday in the den-TV-rock-playroom.

Freddy Junior sat on the floor, his back braced against the couch, his head in his hands. John Henry was stretched out near him with his head between his paws. Each time Freddy Junior moaned, John Henry growled.

Freddy Senior perched at the end of the couch. He plunked reading glasses on the end of his nose and peered through them at the papers on his lap and on the coffee table in front of him.

Lucy lay back in the reclining armchair with a wet towel over her eyes.

And Bunny danced happily back and forth, occasionally clapping her hands together or biting a knuckle.

"So you think it would pay to rent, then. Not to sell," her father said to the coffee table.

"Freddy, if you figure the most we'd be there is a year, I don't see the point of selling, do you?" her mother said from under the wet towel. "Let's rent it, just the way it is."

Freddy Junior moaned loudly from where he was slouched on the floor.

"Grrrrr," John Henry said.

"Okay," Freddy Senior said, and made several check marks on one of his papers. "We'd better call the realtors."

"Now?" Lucy asked.

"Sure. Right now. We barely have two weeks!"

"Ohhh!" Freddy Junior groaned.

"Grrrrr," John Henry responded.

"Don't push it, you free-loading mutt," Freddy Junior warned.

"He's a sweetie," Bunny said, and scratched John Henry's ears. "He's just sorry to see us go, aren't you, John Henry?" The dog raised his head and licked Bunny's hand.

"And the schools. We'll have to notify Bunny's and Freddy's schools."

"We can do that on Monday," Lucy sighed.

"Check."

"I'll pack my dolls now!" Bunny squealed happily.

Freddy Junior began to whimper.

"Freddy, stop that!" his mother said. "If anyone's going to moan, I'll be the one. You kids go to your rooms and decide what you're going to pack."

"Goody!" Bunny cried. "Freddy, can I take John Henry with me?"

"Please," her brother muttered.

Freddy Senior looked up from his papers. "I'll keep on with these lists of whom I'm going to have to see this week. And Lucy?"

"Yes?"

"You'd better call the realtor."

7

Mrs. Millsop, the real estate broker, stood in the middle of the kitchen.

"Of course," she said, "*all* your appliances are in working order, correct?"

"Uh, well, the dishwasher doesn't rinse," Lucy said.

"It *what?*"

"Well, it doesn't rinse. I mean, it washes all right, but something happens in the rinse cycle. You can bang it and that sometimes does it, but mostly, I just take the dishes out and—"

"Have it fixed right away," Mrs. Millsop said. She pointed to the sink with her pencil. "And that faucet is dripping."

"We don't mind," Lucy said. "You can't hear it upstairs in the bedrooms—"

"The renters pay for the utilities and they won't want to pay extra for the water loss. Fix it, please, Mrs. Squill. Now, do you plan to have the yard work done or will you leave it to the renters? Because renters don't care about your lawn, you know, Mrs. Squill, and you might not like what you find when you return."

"Freddy Junior always—" Lucy began and then sighed. "I'll get one of his friends to see to it."

"Fine. Is your furnace cleaned?"

"Uh—"

"Have it cleaned, Mrs. Squill. You don't want to take any chances with the furnace!"

"No," Lucy mumbled and mopped her forehead.

"You'll also have to decide"—Mrs. Millsop jabbed at the cabinets with her pencil—"what pots and pans and kitchen utensils you'll be taking, and you'd better do that right away so I can inform the prospective tenants what they themselves will need to bring—"

"Uh-huh," Lucy said weakly.

"*Now!*" Mrs. Millsop said brightly, "let's move on to the bedrooms!"

"Marvelle," Freddy pleaded, "please *please* ask your parents if you can keep Suzie for me. It'll only be for a year"—his voice cracked—"and that way at least I'll know my two favorite girls are back home waiting for me. . . . "

"Gosh, Freddy, you know how Daddy hates it when you even *park* it here. . . . " Marvelle ran a shiny red nail along Suzie's hood.

"Well, yeah, but—"

"I mean, the red-and-yellow fenders and all . . . You know, we can't put it in the garage, because that's where Daddy's car goes. So that means it would have to sit out here where all the neighbors would see it. . . . "

"Well, gee, Marvelle, I thought you liked Suzie. I was under the impression you thought Suzie was a pretty wonderful car. I mean, you always said how that crazy mutt of yours *loves* to ride in her—"

"Don't you call John Henry a crazy mutt! And really, Freddy, going away for a whole *year*! I mean, Freddy, what about the Christmas parties? And New Year's Eve? What about New Year's *Eve,* Freddy? And what about the Junior *Prom*?"

"Marvelle, I'm going away for a whole year and all you can think about is the *Junior Prom*?"

Bunny rocked back and forth on her skateboard as Ruthie and Geraldine looked up at her from their spot on the grass.

"You're so lucky, Bunny," Ruthie breathed. "Imagine—learning to play polo from Prince Charles!"

"She's just making that up, Ruthie," Geraldine snapped. "Just because her father's business is taking him to London for a year doesn't mean Prince Charles is going to teach her to play polo! She probably won't even *see* anybody in the royal family."

"I will, too," Bunny said. "That's what the families of important Americans do when they're in London, didn't you know that?"

"Only movie stars," Geraldine sniffed.

Bunny frowned and gritted her teeth. "It's all arranged," she said. The only times Bunny ever fibbed were when Geraldine made her angry. "My father told me." Besides, it could still happen, even though it hadn't been offically organized yet. She crossed her fingers behind her back.

"What did your father tell you?"

"That we're meeting the royal family. Mr. McBundy, that Englishman from the toffee company, he arranged it because he thinks my father is the most terrific businessman in America! He said so! He told my father's boss, Mr. Burnside. So there!"

Geraldine looked up at her. "Take a picture," she snorted, "and send it to me. Then I'll believe it."

Bunny's face turned red. She felt the heat on the back of her neck. "I won't have to," she said. "You can see the picture in the newspaper! And then you can show it to that great big portrait of your great-grandfather!"

Sunday, Monday, Tuesday. The week seemed to fly for the Squills and still, there was never enough time in a day.

Lucy needed a replacement at the nursery school. Freddy Senior had work to wind up, most of which he tried to do at home so he could help the rest of the family decide what should go and what should stay, as well as guide all the workmen who came to the house to fix things.

"Did you see the plumber's bill?" he wailed to Lucy, who was busy sorting dishes.

"Forget the plumber," she said. "The people who cleaned the septic tank charged more. And someone's coming to fix the dehumidifier. Mrs. Millsop says if we don't fix it, mold and mildew will eat their way up the stairs and meet us at the door when we come home! By the way, which mover did you call?"

"Me? I thought *you* were calling the movers!"

"Oh, no..."

Freddy Senior patted his wife's shoulder. "It's

okay," he said. "We'll get it all done somehow. And look at the bright side: Once we're in London, we'll never have to see Mrs. Millsop again!"

Wednesday.

The front door slammed.

"Bunny?" Lucy called. "Did you get to the drugstore?"

"It's not *Bunny*!" Freddy Junior yelled. Then he opened the front door and slammed it again.

His mother came into the living room.

"Okay," she said, "what's wrong?"

"*Only* that Marvelle and I are *through*!" Freddy growled. "*Only* that."

"Only that?"

"*And* I can't find the proper owner for Suzie—"

"The *proper*—"

"You know, Mom!" Freddy Junior wailed. "Someone who loves her like I do! Herbie Farnsworth said he'd take her back if I paid *him* fifty bucks!"

"Aw, Freddy . . ."

"I just hope you and Dad are happy," Freddy snarled, "because my whole life is ruined!"

"Oh, now, Freddy, stop that," Lucy said, but Freddy ran up the stairs, moaning, "ruined, ruined" all the way.

Thursday. Mrs. Millsop stood in Freddy Junior's room and looked around.

"Well," she said, "now that your son has taken all the posters off his walls, I'm afraid you're going to have to paint."

"Paint?" Lucy asked as she swallowed an aspirin.

Mrs. Millsop nodded. "See those faded squares on the walls where the posters hung? They look just awful!"

"Well..." Lucy bit her lip. "Maybe we'll just use Freddy's room as our own private storage room instead of the basement..."

But Mrs. Millsop shook her head. "No, that won't do," she said. "Prospective tenants will want the bedroom. And by the way, I've got three couples coming through this evening."

"Oh..."

On Friday, Bunny went to school.

"I'm sorry I missed so much work, Mrs. Pinfish," she said. "But I've been helping my family get ready to move."

"I know, Bunny. Your mother called. Now, take your seat and use the time you have left to—"

"I've been packing and shopping."

"I know, Bunny—"

"But I've been working, too! I've been reading all about England!"

"Well, that's—"

"Their school day is a lot longer than ours, did you know that? Their year is longer, too. So when I come back, I should know a whole lot! I won't be behind at all! I don't mind all that extra school, but you should hear my brother!"

"Bunny, please sit down," Mrs. Pinfish said.

Bunny sat, but she kept on talking. "Freddy says he's lost his girl, he's lost his car, he has to spend a whole year inside some school—"

"Bunny—"

"But I told him, 'Don't worry!' When he's sitting inside Buckingham Palace—"

"*Bunny!*" her classmates yelled all together.

On Sunday evening, the older Squills collapsed in the living room.

"I'm exhausted," Lucy said.

"Me, too," her husband agreed.

"I feel great!" Bunny said. "And we still have all next week to do last-minute stuff!"

"Like find the right tenant," her mother sighed.

"And see where we'll be staying over there," her father added.

"I'm sure Mr. Burnside will fill you in on that

part of it when he comes back," Lucy said. "When is he due back, anyway?"

Freddy Senior looked at his watch. "I'd say any time now. I imagine he'll call as soon as he gets home."

"I hope so. I'm anxious for more details. The flight's all booked, isn't it?"

"All booked. But we have to get up at around four-thirty in the morning."

"Four—?"

"—thirty in the morning. It was the best I could get. Anyway, I didn't want us arriving in the dark of night when everything would be closed and—"

"The phone," Lucy interrupted. "The phone's ringing."

"Maybe it's Mr. Burnside."

"I'll get it!" Bunny sang from the kitchen. There was a moment of silence. Then: "Dad-dy! Guess who? Mr. Burnside!"

Her father bolted for the kitchen.

Bunny held the receiver with her hand over the mouthpiece.

"He wants to know if you took care of the booking for the fourth," she whispered excitedly. "I told him you did!"

"Okay. Give me the phone." Her father held out his hand.

"I told him how excited we were"

"Good, Bun. Give me the phone."

"But he doesn't sound so excited. Why do you think that is? Oh, I guess because he's not the one going—"

"Bunny! Give me the—"

"Here!" She handed it to him and hopped around him as he gripped it and began to talk.

"Harvey? Yes! Hi to you, too! How was the—It was? You did?"

Lucy came into the kitchen and stood next to him, straining to hear the conversation.

Freddy Senior leaned toward her and whispered, "He says they only got one duck the whole week."

"That's one duck too many," Lucy said, making a face.

Her husband listened some more, then whispered again. "He had a good time, though. The client signed the contract."

Lucy nodded and mouthed, "That's good."

"Listen, Harvey," Freddy Senior said into the phone, "about the fourth ... I did manage to get almost everything done and we are ready to go on the fourth—" He listened, smiled, and nodded at his wife. "But what happens when we arrive?" Now he frowned. "I said—what happens when we arrive? What do you mean, arrive where? What *club*, Harvey? What *club* do you mean?" He suddenly put the phone in his other hand, still frowning at his wife. Bunny began to jitterbug around the kitchen table.

"Golf at the club? What are you talking about, Harvey? I'm trying to find out what we're supposed to do when we arrive at Heathrow. Harvey, what do you *mean*, what do I mean? I'm talking about our arrival at Heathrow Airport! In London!" He held the phone away from his ear a moment, then brought it back. "London, *England*, Harvey! Why do you keep talking about the country club?"

Then there was silence as Freddy Senior listened. He transferred the receiver from one ear to the other and back again. He said, "I see . . . I see . . . I see. . . . "

"What?" his wife whispered. "What do you see? What?"

"Of course I remember the name 'McBundy' from Peterson's Toffee," Freddy Senior said into the phone. "What about him? . . . Of course I remember the golf date you mentioned before you left. You were going to call about it. You *did* call about it? You spoke to Bunny?"

Bunny stopped dancing around the table.

"You made the golf date for *the fourth*?" Freddy Senior said. His eyes widened and his ears reddened. "You wanted me to book us at the country club on the fourth! For *golf*! Golf at the club on the fourth!" He licked his lips. He tapped his foot.

"McBundy hears I'm terrific? At *golf*, right, Harvey? Terrific at *golf*. Uh-huh . . . "

Bunny put her thumb in her mouth.

"Why do I keep repeating everything you say, Harvey?" Freddy Senior said loudly into the phone. "I just want my family to hear it, that's all. Thanks for calling, Harvey. What? Oh. Yes, it's been a quiet week. Good-bye." He hung up. *"BUNNY!"*

Bunny sat on the couch in the living room with her ankles crossed and her hands folded in her lap. She stared at her knees as first her father talked and then her mother. Freddy Junior paced the room around them all.

"—not to mention the money we spent on fixing up the house," her mother was saying. "Not that we didn't need the improvements, but we didn't have to do it all at once!"

"I can probably cancel the paint job," her father said, "and the insulation of the attic. Freddy Junior and I can do that ourselves over the next month. But the guys on the roof have already started!"

"And I have to get my job back at the nursery school," Lucy said. "Or some *other* job. And fast, too! And we have to unpack all that stuff we crated up and stored in the basement. . . . "

Bunny's lip quivered as they went on and on. They weren't going to London. They weren't going on an airplane. They wouldn't see the Changing of the Guard and she probably would never get to meet the Queen or learn polo from the Prince of Wales. All "the fourth" meant now was a golf date. For her father and Mr. McBundy and Mr. Burnside and someone else. A golf date. Mr. Burnside had been talking about a golf date and Bunny had decided he'd been talking about their trip. Their whole house had been turned upside down because Bunny had talked again instead of listening.

But the worst was yet to come!

She was going back to school. Back to Mrs. Pinfish's fifth grade. Not only had she missed a whole week's work that would have to be made up, but she had to face Ruthie. And Mary Ann. And Helen. And . . .

Geraldine.

Bunny twisted her hands in her lap. She looked up into the faces of her tired and angry parents. Then she looked at her brother pacing the room. All of them had turned over their lives in one week because she had talked too much, and now they were going to have to spend a lot of time getting everything back in order.

Including herself.

All my fault, Bunny said to herself.

"All my fault," she said out loud as two large tears trickled down her cheeks.

"Yeah, it sure is!" Freddy Junior bellowed at her. "I get to keep Suzie, but what's going to happen with *Marvelle?*"

And the plumber and painter and mover, Freddy Senior thought.

And Mrs. Millsop! Lucy thought.

And Geraldine Pennywhistle, Bunny thought. All my fault. Bigmouth!

"Hmph," Geraldine Pennywhistle sniffed. "Here comes Bunny. As if Monday mornings weren't bad enough."

"Don't be mean," Helen said, straightening the schoolbooks in her arms. "She's just excited about moving to London. Anybody would be excited about that."

"I know," Geraldine said, "but if I hear another word about her baby-sitting for Princess Diana's kids, I'm going to—"

"Sh!" Ruthie said. "Here she comes. Hi, Bunny!"

"H'lo," Bunny said, and kept on walking toward the front door of the school.

The girls looked at each other.

"Hey! Bunny!" Ruthie caught up with her. "Aren't you getting ready to leave? I didn't think you'd be in school at all this week."

"Oh," Bunny said, "well... I will be. We're, uh, not going."

"Not going? Not going to London?" Ruthie cried and Geraldine and Helen ran up to them.

"What do you mean, you're not going?" Geraldine asked.

"Not going now or not going at all?" Helen asked.

"Um..." Bunny said.

"Come on, let's have it," Geraldine said. "What happened?"

"Well, we just... uh...," Bunny stammered.

"Come on, come on," Geraldine pushed. "What's the story?"

But Bunny, looking miserable, kept on walking.

"Hey, how come you're not babbling, Squill?" Geraldine insisted, matching Bunny's stride. "Where's all the talk-talk-talk? What about your picture in the papers, and Prince Charles and the Tower of London and your graduating from Oxford and Cambridge and—"

"Quiet, Geraldine," Helen said. "Come on, Bunny. Tell us what happened."

But Bunny just shook her head and went through the school door.

It didn't take long for everyone to find out, though. The high school heard about it from Freddy Junior, who, following Marvelle Maloney through the halls, spilled everything.

"It was Bunny!" he wailed at her. "It was all my sister's fault for thinking a *golf date* was the day we'd all fly to *England!*"

"I don't care," Marvelle said, her nose in the air. "You called John Henry a crazy mutt and you said I was shallow for only thinking about parties!"

"I was upset, Marvelle," Freddy argued. "Can't you understand I was only upset about leaving? And we were never leaving at all! Bunny got the whole thing wrong! Listen, Marvelle, I'll be *here* for the Junior Prom. . . . "

"It's too late," Marvelle said firmly.

"It's too late," Lucy Squill said, as Bunny looked up at her tearfully. "You should have thought of that before you had us all running around like rabbits. I've told you and told you to listen before you talk, but now you've really done it, Bunny."

"But maybe you'll learn something from all this," Freddy Senior said. "From now on, maybe you'll hear what other people have to say before you go flying off in all directions."

"And," Freddy Junior added when his parents had left the room, "keep your mouth shut or I'll make the dentist wire your jaws and glue your lips together!" He shook his fist at Bunny and clomped upstairs to his room.

Slowly, the Squills got their house back in order. They carried crates and cartons up from the basement, unpacked them, and put all their contents back in drawers, closets, cabinets, and on shelves. Freddy put his posters back on the walls, covering the faded squares; Lucy managed to get her job back—the nursery school had been able to get only a substitute; Freddy Senior straightened things out with the bank, the realtor, the phone company, the movers, and all his clients. Bunny caught up with her schoolwork and put away all the flyers, books, and brochures about England.

But she did it all silently. Hardly a word escaped her lips.

"How was your day, Bunny?" her mother would ask after school.

"Mmm . . ."

"What?"

"Okay . . ."

"How are the girls? Helen? Ruthie? Mary Ann?"

"Fine..."

"How's Geraldine?"

"Mmm."

Freddy Senior had his golf date, and he and Harvey Burnside won their match from Mr. Mc-Bundy and the other man from Peterson's Olde English Toffee. Mr. McBundy didn't seem at all pleased, and Mr. Burnside wondered privately to Freddy Senior if they'd get the account after all.

"I don't think I could go through all that packing and arranging again, anyway," Freddy Senior sighed.

And things began to return to normal.

Almost.

"Have you noticed how quiet things are around here?" Lucy asked Freddy Junior one afternoon.

"Yeah," he answered. "It's nice."

"Well... it is and it isn't," his mother said. "Bunny doesn't sing anymore, she doesn't laugh—"

"—and she doesn't talk!" Freddy Junior finished. "I like it."

"I don't like it," Freddy Senior said, when a few weeks had gone by. "She's too quiet."

"I know," his wife sighed. "She doesn't even plan things with her friends anymore. She's never on the phone...."

"And our breakfasts and dinners—all you can hear are clinking glasses and forks!"

"I always wanted peace and quiet after a day of teaching," Lucy said, "but now I'm not so sure."

"Bunny?" Mrs. Pinfish said during English. "Have you read the story?"

Bunny nodded.

"I can't hear you," Mrs. Pinfish said, raising her voice.

Bunny nodded harder.

"That's not what I meant, Bunny. I'd like you to answer me, please."

"Mrs. Pinfish never said *that* before," Geraldine whispered to Ruthie.

Mrs. Pinfish frowned. "Bunny Squill, any other time you'd have told me the whole story, its author, and the author's entire life before I could even get the question out of my mouth."

Geraldine giggled and Mrs. Pinfish scowled at her.

"Bunny," she said, "I'd like to see you at lunchtime."

Bunny nodded and sighed.

"Bunny," Mrs. Pinfish said when they were alone in the classroom, "I'm starting to get worried about you."

Bunny blinked.

"I don't like this sudden change in you. I know you've learned a lesson from what happened . . . "

Bunny nodded.

" . . . and I think it's time for you to get over that and recover your spirits. You know now that there's a time to talk and a time to listen, but being absolutely silent all the time isn't what anyone wants." Mrs. Pinfish smiled.

"But it is," Bunny said. "It is what everyone wants. And they're right, Mrs. Pinfish. Whenever I talk I get into trouble and people get mad. So I'm not going to say anything anymore. Ever!"

"Bunny, there is a middle ground," Mrs. Pinfish said.

But Bunny shook her head. "No," she insisted, "every time I open my mouth there's trouble. So it stays closed."

No one thought it would last.

"She'll talk," Geraldine told the girls. "She'll talk as much as ever. *More.* You'll see."

"I wish she would," Ruthie said. "She just doesn't seem like Bunny anymore. It's like there's another person inside that body."

"Yeah," Helen sighed. "Bunny's face, Bunny's clothes, but no Bunny inside."

"I miss her," Mary Ann said.

"I do, too," Ruthie agreed.

"Miss her! Miss Bunny? Shrill Squill? That voice always yammering, singing, giggling, talk-talk-talking? *Miss* her?"

"*Yes*, Geraldine, we do!" the girls chorused.

"Me, too," Geraldine muttered.

Everyone tried.

Now Geraldine waited for Bunny to leave her house in the mornings on her way to school and she'd hurry down Pennywhistle Lane to catch up with her.

"Bunny! Hi!" Geraldine called brightly.

Bunny glanced at Geraldine and kept on walking.

"It's almost Halloween, Bunny. Shall we go out together this year? Shall we trick-or-treat with Ruthie or by ourselves?"

Bunny shrugged and kept walking.

"What are you going to be? I think *I'm* going to go as a princess!" Whoops, Geraldine thought. Let's not talk about princesses! "Well, maybe I'll be a witch. What about you, Bunny?" She nudged Bunny with her elbow. "Come on, Squill. What costume are you going to wear?"

But Bunny just shrugged again, and Geraldine sighed.

"It's no use, Mrs. Squill. I tried," Geraldine told Lucy when they met one afternoon between their houses. "I keep trying. So does Mrs. Pinfish, and the other girls. But Bunny hardly says anything. She doesn't talk, she doesn't sing, she doesn't even *hum* anymore!"

Lucy shook her head. "I know, Geraldine. The other night, her father and I had a long talk with her about when to talk, when to listen, how to compromise! That is, *we* talked. She just sat there."

"Looking sad and mopey?"

"Looking sad and mopey."

"She wouldn't go out with us on Halloween," Geraldine said. "Maybe she'll perk up for Thanksgiving."

Freddy Junior looked up from his math book when he heard the knock on his door. Hey, he thought with a smile, maybe it's Bunny! Then he clicked his tongue.

"Why should I be happy about that!" he said aloud. Then he called, "Yo!"

His parents came into his room together.

"I didn't do anything," Freddy said with a frown.

"Now, Freddy, do you think your parents only visit you in your room to scold you about something?"

"Yes . . . ," Freddy Junior said warily. "Is this a quiz?"

"No, it's not a quiz! And we didn't come in because we think you've done something wrong," his father said. "Have you?"

Freddy chewed his lip. "I don't think so," he said.

"How's the car?" Lucy asked.

"Gee, I'm glad you asked," Freddy Junior said, brightening. "I think now that the weather's getting colder, Suzie's going to have an even bigger problem starting up. So I was thinking . . . maybe I could keep her in the garage? Dad?"

"How about a nice warm blanket at night?" his father suggested.

"I tried that."

"Well, actually, Freddy, there's something else we'd like you to try," his mother said. "It's about Bunny."

"What about her?"

"We think you're our last resort. You know how she looks up to you. . . . "

"Who, *Bunny?*"

"She does," his father confirmed. "She always has. Little sisters are like that. Anyway, we were hoping that you could bring her out of this funk she's in. . . . "

"I *like* the funk she's in," Freddy Junior said gruffly. "She doesn't talk anymore. Now if only Marvelle were still my girlfriend, we could enjoy the peace and quiet!"

"Freddy, we're worried about Bunny," his mother said.

"We really are, son. We need something to snap her out of this."

Freddy Junior nodded. "Yeah," he admitted, "I guess we do. I used to bug her all the time about her talking, but now I don't have anything to bug her about. And that bugs me! What did you have in mind?"

"Well . . . ," his father began, "how about offering to take her for a ride in Suzie? Maybe to the movies or out for an ice cream or something? I think it would do wonders for Bunny if her big brother asked her to go out in his car for an afternoon."

"You do?" Freddy Junior asked. "You think that would do it? Bunny would be her old self again?"

"I don't know about her old self," Lucy said, "but

maybe a happier self than she's been. She just went from one extreme to the other, and neither one is good. We need to get Bunny off her seesaw and back on some level ground. Will you give it a try, son?"

"Sure," Freddy said and smiled in spite of himself when his mother hugged him.

Freddy Junior swaggered into the kitchen where Bunny was peeling potatoes for supper.

"Hi!" he said, and clopped Bunny on the shoulder. She swayed slightly beneath the clop and nodded at her brother.

"What're you doing?" Freddy asked.

Bunny held up the peeler and a potato.

"Uh-*huh*," Freddy said. "Listen, little sister, I have something better for you to do than *that*."

Bunny looked at him and went back to scraping potato skins.

"Don't you want to hear what it is?" Freddy asked.

Bunny shook her head.

"Aw, come on, Bun!" Freddy couldn't believe it. He could never remember a time in his life when his sister ignored him.

"Listen," he said, leaning toward her over the table, "I've got Suzie all warmed up and we both want to take you out for a ride. And maybe downtown for an ice cream. What do you say to *that*?"

He grinned at Bunny and waited for her to be thrilled.

Bunny sighed. Bunny shrugged. Bunny went on peeling.

"Bunny?" Freddy said. "Did you *hear* me?"

Bunny nodded.

"You're not coming? Do I understand you to mean," Freddy Junior said slowly, "that you are not coming? You don't want a ride in my car? You don't want an ice cream? Two things you would have given me your year's allowance for just a few months ago?"

Bunny nodded.

Freddy Junior went to his room in a daze.

At Thanksgiving dinner, Bunny ate a lot of turkey, a lot of cranberry sauce, a lot of mashed potatoes, a lot of salad, and a lot of homemade bread, but she didn't say the Thanksgiving prayer—at least, out loud—and she didn't spend the dinner listing for everyone all the things she had to be thankful for.

"We have to do something," Lucy told Freddy Senior.

They had a meeting.

As soon as Thanksgiving vacation was over, they met one evening in Mrs. Pinfish's room at the elementary school: three Squills, Geraldine, Mary Ann, Helen, Ruthie, and the teacher.

"She did answer a question today," Mrs. Pinfish told the group. "I was so thrilled to see her hand raised, I called on her right away."

"Yeah," Geraldine chimed in. "The right answer was 'Saturn.' And that's just what Bunny said. 'Saturn.' "

"Not: 'Saturn: the sixth planet from the sun and second largest in the solar system, encircled by ten satellites and a system of narrow rings composed of ice-covered particles. Mean distance from the sun: eight hundred and eighty-six million · miles,' " Ruthie said, and exhaled. "Whew!"

"That was very good, Ruthie," Mrs. Pinfish exclaimed.

"Well . . . that's what Bunny would have said. The *old* Bunny, I mean. . . . "

"Yes, that's what she would have said all right," Mrs. Pinfish agreed. "And I'm glad we decided to have this meeting tonight, because I have an idea— something that may just do the trick! Now all of you know that fifth grade is the year the children become eligible to perform in the Christmas Concert and—"

"*Bunny?*" Freddy Junior interrupted. "In the Christmas Concert? The voice that would drive the Three Wise Men back the way they came?"

Geraldine snorted loudly. "Now, don't be nasty, Freddy."

"Look who's talking about being nasty, Pennywhistle!" Freddy Junior retorted.

"Now, stop that," Mrs. Pinfish said at the same time his parents said, "Fred-dy!"

So everybody stopped talking and Mrs. Pinfish began.

9

"Who, me?" Bunny asked, studying her fingernails.

"It was your teacher's idea," Lucy told her. "You have a lovely voice."

"Well, you sing in tune, anyway," her brother said.

"I sure would be proud, seeing you up there in one of those pretty robes," her father said.

Bunny looked at them.

"Me, too," Freddy Junior said, and then added, "No kidding."

"I don't want to," Bunny said.

'Come on, Bunny," Geraldine said, pulling at Bunny's arm. "Let's go."

100

"No."

"You won't get in if you don't audition. You have to go. This is the last day."

"No," Bunny said.

"All right, then," Geraldine said. "I'll go by myself. How does this sound: Si-i-lent ni-ght . . . Ho-oo-oly ni-iight," she croaked.

Bunny giggled.

"See? I'm terrible. Are you going to let me make a fool of myself or are you going to be the representative of our fifth grade?"

"How come you're being so nice to me, Geraldine?" Bunny asked. "You never liked the way I sang before. . . ."

"I'm not being nice, Squill!" Geraldine snapped. "I just think our class ought to send its best people, that's all!"

"Where do you think you're going, Bunny?" Mary Ann and Ruthie appeared on each side of her.

"Home . . . I guess. . . ."

"You can go home if you want," Mary Ann said.

"But first, we're going over to the high school," Ruthie finished.

"And we're not taking no for an answer."

"You can decide on the way what you're going to sing."

A car pulled up at the curb. It coughed, sputtered, coughed again, and then wheezed as it idled.

"Here's your chauffeur," Ruthie said. "Hi, Freddy!"

"Hop in," Freddy Junior said, and leaned over to open Suzie's door. "All of you."

Bunny walked down to the choirmaster, seated in the front row of the auditorium. She glanced once at her brother and her friends who were standing in the back.

"Name, please?" the man said.

"Uh, Bunny Squill."

"Age?"

"Ten."

"Ah, your first year, then."

Bunny cleared her throat. "Yes," she said.

"What would you like to sing, Bunny?"

" 'O Little Town of Bethlehem.' "

"Good choice." He nodded at the pianist, who gave Bunny an introduction. "O lit-tle—" Bunny began, and stopped.

"Wrong key," the pianist said, and played another introduction. "Go on, Bunny. Start again." But Bunny just stood there.

In the back, Geraldine bit her lip. Mary Ann, Ruthie, and Helen crossed their fingers. Mrs. Pinfish slipped into the last seat in the last row and held her breath. Freddy Junior muttered under his breath, "Come on, Bun. . . . "

Bunny raised her eyes. She looked around at the accompanist. She looked at the choirmaster. She cleared her throat again. "Okay," she said at last. "Start it again, please." And she sang.

It wasn't her usual full, bell-like singing voice, but it wasn't the small mumble she'd been using lately, either. The little crowd, pulling for her in the back, could hear all the words. And she did stay in tune. The carol sounded—

"Pretty," Helen whispered to Geraldine, who answered, "It was okay."

And when Bunny walked back up the aisle, Freddy Junior said, "Yeah, well, not bad," and put a hand on her shoulder as they walked to the car.

The next day, the names of the elementary school members of the Christmas Concert Choir were posted on the bulletin board outside the principal's office.

"You made it, Bunny!" Geraldine cried as she peered at the list. "You and Willie Harrigan! You two are the only fifth-graders! Good for you, Bunny, we knew you could do it!"

"Congratulations, Bunny!" Mrs. Pinfish said, smiling at her.

"Yay, Bunny!" the class cheered.

"Thanks," Bunny said.

Christmas was only three weeks away, so the choir rehearsals were held every day after school. The solo performers worked on their own, as well as with the two music teachers, but the choir hàd a more difficult job to do. They had many harmony lines and rhythms to learn. The choirmaster was strict, and he knew just what he wanted from his group.

"Let me hear that line again," he called, tapping his baton. "Just the altos. Ready?" He gave them a downbeat.

"An-gels we have heard on high," they sang, "sweet-ly sing-ing o'er the plains..."

"Wait," the choirmaster said. "You're all trying to sing so loudly, you're missing your notes as well as drowning out the others." He lifted his baton and pointed to Bunny, directly in front of him in the front row. "You," he said. "What's your name?"

Bunny's face reddened. "Bunny Squill," she said, almost whispering.

"Honey Squill, here," the choirmaster said to the group, "is probably our youngest member and she seems to be the only one paying attention. Let's hear your line, Honey."

Bunny didn't correct him about her name, but she sang the alto line clearly.

"Ah, you see?" the choirmaster said. "Honey, here, was"—he held his hand up to his ear—"listening! Very important! Not just singing to hear her own voice, but listening to the others to make a good blend! Thank you, Honey."

Bunny looked at him, blinked, and nodded.

"How was choir practice today, Bunny?" her mother asked at supper.

"Good," Bunny answered, and helped herself to more meat loaf.

Geraldine huddled inside her down jacket and wrapped her scarf twice around her neck. "We hardly get to see you anymore, Bunny. You're always at practice. Is it fun?"

"Uh-huh."

"Better wrap your scarf around again, too. You have to protect your throat. Don't want to get laryngitis, right?"

"Uh-huh."

"Gee, it's getting cold, isn't it, Bunny?"

"Uh-huh . . . " Bunny looked up as she tugged at her scarf and discovered that the wind had turned the street sign around. The words "Pennywhistle Lane" were now facing the other way so that a stranger couldn't tell what street he was on. But Bunny didn't tell that to Geraldine.

"You, over there. The girl with the red hair," the choirmaster said, pointing to a tall ninth-grader. "Go stand over there next to what's-her-name, Honey. Listen to how she holds a line."

The red-haired girl, whose face now matched her hair, stepped down to the front row.

"All right, let's hear the altos," the choirmaster said.

The red-haired girl opened her mouth and made a face. "That's wrong," she said.

"Just listen for a minute," Bunny told her. "Don't try to sing."

The altos sang their line again. The red-haired girl bent down and Bunny sang right into her ear.

"Now ask the piano player to play the line for you," Bunny whispered. "And just listen to it over and over before you sing. Then you'll know it. But the real trick is to be able to hold that line while you're listening to the others." She looked up at the red-haired girl and smiled. "I'll stay after and sing it with you if you like," Bunny offered. "And I know the soprano part, so we can make doubly sure you've got it."

"Well, thanks," the redhead said. "How old are you?"

"Ten," Bunny answered.

"Ten, huh? How'd you learn all that music? And the soprano part, too?"

"From listening," Bunny answered.

"Where is she?" Lucy whispered to Freddy Senior. "I can't find her."

"Right there." He pointed. "Front row."

"Oh, yes." She weaved back and forth in her seat to get a better view.

The whole town always came to the Christmas Concert—even people who had no children participating. It was a tradition, and even old Grandpa Farnsworth, who complained the entire time about his rheumatism, wouldn't miss it. The auditorium was packed.

It was a full program. Barbara-Sue Ardmore, who had studied elocution for a whole year, recited the story of the birth of the Christ child, and an appropriately costumed group from the seventh grade mimed it while she narrated.

Arthur Greevey, who was thirteen and a half but whose voice hadn't changed yet, sang "The Little Drummer Boy" a cappella.

"The First Noël" was sung by a graduating senior, Alice Beazely, accompanied by Andrew Hardee on the accordion.

Carmen Ortiz from the tenth grade played two solos on the piano whose titles no one knew.

And interspersed between these numbers, the Christmas Choir sang. They wore silky gray robes with big pink bowties at their necks, and their flushed faces matched the color of the ties.

Finally, it was time for the last song. The choir was to close the concert with their rendition of "Angels We Have Heard on High," the choirmaster's favorite. He tapped his baton, nodded, and smiled at the group. He raised his arms, brought them down.

"An-gels we have heard on high," they sang.

Bunny looked out over the darkened auditorium as she sang. She dropped her jaw as she had been taught in order to make a rounder, clearer sound.

She could hardly hear herself, but she knew she was holding her line, singing the words correctly. All around her, voices were raised in the beautiful carol.

" . . . Ech-o-ing their joy-ous strains. Glo—ri—a, in ex-cel-sis De-o . . . "

Bunny's eyes glistened as she sang.

" . . . In ex-celsis, De—e—o. Ahh—men."

The audience was silent for almost a quarter of a minute. Then they broke into applause. The choir glowed from the stage.

"Bunny!" Lucy's eyes were brimming. "You were wonderful!"

"Yeah," Freddy Junior said. "Listen, I'm going to go congratulate Marvelle, okay?"

"What for?" Freddy Senior asked. "She didn't do anything in the concert."

"I know," Freddy Junior said, "but she looks great in her Christmas outfit." He began to push his way through the crowd.

"You really were terrific, sweetheart," Freddy Senior said, bending down to hug his daughter. "You just stood right out."

"No, I didn't, Daddy," Bunny said. "I didn't stand out. That was the point. I blended in. We all listened to each other and we all became one as we sang. That's what the choirmaster said. Nobody stood out and that's the way it's supposed to be."

"Ahh," her father said. "Right."

"When you're a soloist, then you stand out. But when you're not, you're part of a group and you're working toward the same goal."

"I see," Lucy said.

At that moment, the choirmaster passed them on his way to the cafeteria for the Christmas party.

"Thanks for your hard work, Honey," he said, tapping Bunny on the shoulder.

"You're welcome," she answered, "and it's 'Bunny.' Bunny Squill." She looked up at her parents. "I think I'll find Geraldine," she said, "and get her some punch. You know, maybe Geraldine and the others would like to form a singing group. Maybe over Christmas vacation we could get together and I could teach—" She clapped a hand over her own mouth, then removed it slowly. "Just some punch," she said, and smiled. "Geraldine will like that."